Welcome to Rose-Petal Place!

I'm Elmer the elm tree, and I know everything there is to know about this beautiful garden because I keep it all recorded in my diary. Let me introduce you to the delightful group of characters who have made Rose-Petal Place their home.

Rose-Petal is the natural leader and protector of Rose-Petal Place. She is as talented as she is beautiful and sweet. Her magical singing keeps the garden blooming, and her good common sense keeps everyone in it safe and happy.

Sunny Sunflower is Rose-Petal's best friend. As is often the case with best friends, they are opposites in many ways. Sunny is a tomboy who always says exactly what's on her mind. You might say she's "spice" to Rose-Petal's "sugar."

Lily Fair is a dreamer whose dearest wish is to be a star. She is sincere and dedicated and can be seen practicing her dancing at all hours of the day and night.

Daffodil is all business. She runs the Bouquet Boutique, where all the girls go for their beautiful clothes. She has big plans for her future as a businesswoman and is never without her flower-shaped calculator.

Orchid is Daffodil's best customer. She loves to pamper herself and spends most of her time on self-improvement. When Orchid is not actually shopping, she is thinking about it!

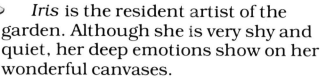*Iris* is the resident artist of the garden. Although she is very shy and quiet, her deep emotions show on her wonderful canvases.

Pitterpat is a fluffy and devoted kitten. She and Rose-Petal have an extra-special relationship and are rarely seen apart. Pitterpat has saved Rose-Petal from trouble on more than one occasion.

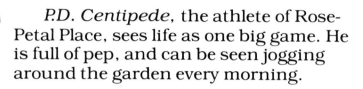*P.D. Centipede*, the athlete of Rose-Petal Place, sees life as one big game. He is full of pep, and can be seen jogging around the garden every morning.

*Seymour J. Snailsworth* is a snail of great wisdom. He carries his unique and elegant home on his back, and can always be called upon for a word or two of advice.

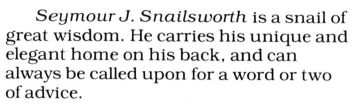*Tumbles the Hedgehog* is a happy-go-lucky fellow who is always full of fun and laughs. The girls love to have Tumbles around, even if he does trip and stumble a lot!

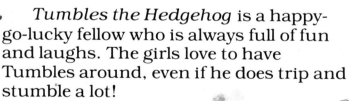Unfortunately, there is a dark and untended part of the garden where nothing grows. There, in Tin-Can Castle, live *Nastina,* an evil spider, and her hateful assistant, *Horace Fly.* Nastina's goal in life is to get rid of Rose-Petal and make herself Queen of Rose-Petal Place. So we are always on our guard against Nastina and her wicked tricks.

With all of us working and playing together, Rose-Petal Place remains an enchanted garden full of sunshine and flowers, music and laughter. Please come join us!

Library of Congress Cataloging in Publication Data: Foslien, Dagmar. The fantastic fashion show. Rose-Petal Place. SUMMARY:
When Rose-Petal and her garden friends plan a fashion show, Nastina the spider is determined to ruin it.
[1. Gardens—Fiction.   2. Flowers—Fiction.   3. Spiders—Fiction.   4. Fashion—Fiction]   I. Title.   II. Series.
PZ7.F79Fan   1984   [E]   83-24933   ISBN 0-910313-50-4
Manufactured in the United States of America 1 2 3 4 5 6 7 8 9 0

ROSE·PETAL·PLACE™

The Fantastic Fashion Show

by Dagmar Foslien
Pictures by Pat Paris and Jeanie Shackelford

 CHILDRENS PRESS CHOICE

A Parker Brothers title selected for educational distribution

ISBN 0-516-09092-5

"I'm bored!" complained Sunny Sunflower, as she drooped on the garden bench.

"There's always a cure for that," smiled Rose-Petal. "Find a new interest, and get involved."

"Really, Rose-Petal, this is serious. I mean it! And I'm not the only one who is bored. The other girls are, too."

For a moment, Rose-Petal stroked the shiny fur of Pitterpat, her kitten. Then she said, "We could have a fashion show."

"In Carnation Hall? With music, guests, and everything? Sounds great!"

"Not so fast," said Rose-Petal. "We must go and talk to the other girls before we make any decision."

"Let's go now," begged Sunny Sunflower impatiently.

Hand in hand, with Pitterpat following closely,
they hurried down the flagstone path to the
white gazebo near the center of Rose-Petal Place.

Orchid, Lily Fair, Iris, and Daffodil were sitting on the steps of the gazebo, taking turns playing catch with P. D. Centipede.

"Guess what! We're going to have a fashion show!" announced Sunny Sunflower.

"That's a great idea! If we do have one, I could manage the whole thing. I know more about clothes than any of you. And besides, I know exactly how a show should be done," said Orchid quickly.

"Some people jump on the train before it's even pulled into the station," muttered Sunny Sunflower.

"You're just jealous of my abilities," sniffed Orchid.

"Orchid, you *are* the best of all!" buzzed Horace Fly, who breezed in just in time to defend his true love, Orchid.

"Get out of here, Horace!" screamed Orchid, as she tried unsuccessfully to swat him with her little handbag.

The girls had many different ideas about the fashion show.

Lily Fair, wearing her blue leotards and matching ballet slippers, danced and posed gracefully before the group. She hoped someone would suggest that she perform during the show.

Iris volunteered to paint posters letting everyone in Rose Petal Place know about the show.

"My experience at the Bouquet Boutique should help, too," declared Daffodil happily. "Let's see. I think we could even make a tidy profit," she added, as she pressed the keys of her flower-shaped calculator to check her figures.

Rose-Petal smiled as she listened to their eager planning.

"Will you sing for the show, Rose-Petal?" asked Sunny Sunflower.

"I will be happy to sing, if Lily Fair will dance." Lily Fair was delighted to agree.

"We'll all be models," said Sunny Sunflower. "I wonder if Seymour J. Snailsworth would be the master of ceremonies. He'd be perfect!"

Meantime, Horace Fly, hurt and angry over Orchid's rejection, flew to the far side of the garden to Tin-Can Castle, the dismal home of Nastina, the evil spider.

"I know something you don't know, Nastina," he buzzed.

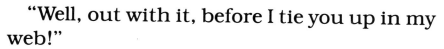

"Well, out with it, before I tie you up in my web!"

"Rose-Petal and her friends are having a fashion show."

"Are you sure?"

"Positively."

"So those little sillies think they know something about fashion! Well, I suppose they'd never invite me to be in their show. They simply don't appreciate my basic black dress!"

"You're absolutely stunning, Nastina," said Horace. But he didn't sound as though he meant it.

But Nastina heard only what she wanted to hear. She posed and turned around and around on her four spidery legs.

All at once she turned to Horace and said, "Go to those girls and tell them I would probably model in their show, if they asked me nicely."

"Your word is my command, Nastina."
As he slowly returned to the gazebo, he
muttered to himself, "This isn't going to be
easy!"

Horace approached Sunny Sunflower with
this proposal: "I have a new model for your
show."

"Who's that?"

"Out of the goodness of her heart, Nastina has
volunteered her services."

"Don't make me laugh! You stay away from
this show, and keep Nastina away too!"

When Horace brought the message to Nastina, she screamed in anger, stamped her many feet, and began plotting her revenge.

"How could they insult me like that! They'll regret it before I'm finished with them," she muttered.

For the next few days, Rose-Petal Place was full of excitement as the girls rushed around planning the fashion show.

Each model chose three lovely costumes to wear.

Pink, lavender, white, orange, yellow, and purple — what a beautiful collection of colors! Rose-Petal said that the girls should be free to choose accessories, so there were jewel-studded belts, glamorous hats, and elegant handbags.

"What can we do to help?" asked P. D. Centipede. He and Tumbles the Hedgehog were feeling left out of all the fun.

"If you two could be serious for a little while, you could decorate Carnation Hall," said Sunny Sunflower.

"We'll be so-o good!" promised P. D.

Seymour J. Snailsworth, who always carried his home with him, moved to the right side of the stage at Carnation Hall. From there he offered suggestions to the two workers.

P. D. and Tumbles worked hard. They hung brightly colored streamers, built a runway for the girls' parade, and lined the stage with baskets of garden flowers.

All the costumes were carefully hung in the dressing rooms backstage in Carnation Hall. Everything was ready.

Tired from all their efforts, the models and their helpers decided to go to bed early. Seymour volunteered to guard Carnation Hall.

Seymour studied the script he had prepared for the fashion show. It had been a long and tiring day. Although he wanted to stay alert, his head nodded, his glasses fell from his nose, and the script fell to the floor. Soon Seymour was fast asleep.

About midnight, two shadowy figures crept into Carnation Hall. They tiptoed past the sleeping guard, and quietly disappeared into the dressing rooms. After a short time, they reappeared and walked quickly and quietly out of the building.

At sunrise, Seymour woke with a start. He looked all around and was relieved to see that everything on the stage seemed all right.

Soon all six girls trooped in.
Sunny Sunflower rushed up to greet Seymour.
"Good morning, Seymour. How's everything?
This show is just so exciting, isn't it?"

They happily danced on into the dressing rooms. Then Seymour heard loud angry screams and cries.

"Who poured this ugly green paint on our lovely gowns?"

"They're all ruined!"

"Who would do such an evil thing?"

"Nastina, that's who!"

"Seymour, was Nastina here?" asked Rose-Petal.

Poor Seymour was so upset he could hardly answer. "I . . . I . . . I . . . fell . . . asleep. . . ."

"Oh, Seymour. Because of you, we won't be able to have the fashion show!" exclaimed Orchid.

Rose-Petal said sternly, "Girls, I'm sure Seymour did his best. Remember that Nastina is unbelievably wicked and tricky. What's done is done. Let's think of something we can do to make the best of a bad situation."

"But the show is ruined," wailed Daffodil.

"Nonsense. Don't any of you say anything about the paint to anyone. What can we do to save the show?"

"Well, we certainly can't wear these gowns," sobbed Orchid.

All at once Rose-Petal smiled. "The show must go on. Let's model swimsuits. The stage must be transformed to a beach setting. I will sing, and Lily Fair will dance."

Rose-Petal's good sense and good humor wo
the day. The girls could even smile as she sang

When you're feeling blue,
And everything is bad,
It's really up to you
To change "bad" to "glad."
So sing this little tune,
Clap your hands in time,
You'll feel better soon
With this happy little rhyme.

Seymour promised to tell his crew, Tumbles and P. D., to change the stage setting, as Rose-Petal had suggested.

Just then, Horace Fly breezed in. "How's your fashion show coming?"

Rose-Petal answered quickly, "Just fine."

With a puzzled expression on his face, Horace went back to report to Nastina.

Sunny Sunflower whispered, "We all know who helped Nastina do her dirty work, don't we? Did you see the paint on his nose?"

By show time a large crowd had come to see the show. They applauded each song, each dance, and each lovely model in her stylish swimsuit. The show was a huge success.

As Rose-Petal prepared to sing her closing
solo, she saw Nastina and Horace peeking
through the flowers. She couldn't resist smiling
as she saw Nastina screaming at Horace.
Then she sang her happy song again:

When you're feeling blue,
And everything is bad,
It's really up to you
To change "bad" to "glad."

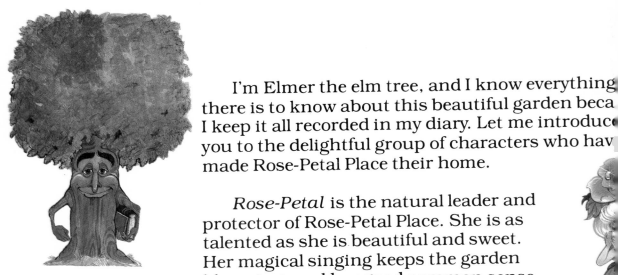

I'm Elmer the elm tree, and I know everything there is to know about this beautiful garden beca I keep it all recorded in my diary. Let me introduce you to the delightful group of characters who hav made Rose-Petal Place their home.

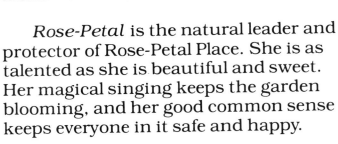

Rose-Petal is the natural leader and protector of Rose-Petal Place. She is as talented as she is beautiful and sweet. Her magical singing keeps the garden blooming, and her good common sense keeps everyone in it safe and happy.

Sunny Sunflower is Rose-Petal's best friend. As is often the case with best friends, they are opposites in many ways. Sunny is a tomboy who always says exactly what's on her mind. You might say she's "spice" to Rose-Petal's "sugar."

Lily Fair is a dreamer whose dearest wish is to be a star. She is sincere and dedicated and can be seen practicing her dancing at all hours of the day and night.

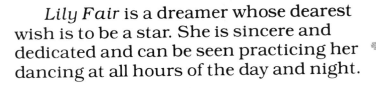

Daffodil is all business. She runs the Bouquet Boutique, where all the girls go for their beautiful clothes. She has big plans for her future as a businesswoman and is never without her flower-shaped calculator.

Orchid is Daffodil's best customer. She loves to pamper herself and spends most of her time on self-improvement. When Orchid is not actually shopping, she is thinking about it!

Iris is the resident artist of the garden. Although she is very shy and quiet, her deep emotions show on her wonderful canvases.

Pitterpat is a fluffy and devoted kitten. She and Rose-Petal have an extra-special relationship and are rarely seen apart. Pitterpat has saved Rose-Petal from trouble on more than one occasion.

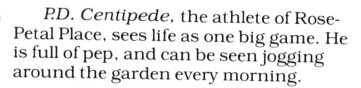

P.D. Centipede, the athlete of Rose-Petal Place, sees life as one big game. He is full of pep, and can be seen jogging around the garden every morning.

Seymour J. Snailsworth is a snail of great wisdom. He carries his unique and elegant home on his back, and can always be called upon for a word or two of advice.

Tumbles the Hedgehog is a happy-go-lucky fellow who is always full of fun and laughs. The girls love to have Tumbles around, even if he does trip and stumble a lot!

Unfortunately, there is a dark and untended part of the garden where nothing grows. There, in Tin-Can Castle, live *Nastina*, an evil spider, and her hateful assistant, *Horace Fly*. Nastina's goal in life is to get rid of Rose-Petal and make herself Queen of Rose-Petal Place. So we are always on our guard against Nastina and her wicked tricks.

With all of us working and playing together, Rose-Petal Place remains an enchanted garden full of sunshine and flowers, music and laughter. Please come join us!